CHIN CHIANG AND THE DRAGON'S DANCE

WRITTEN AND ILLUSTRATED BY
IAN WALLACE

A Groundwood Book

DOUGLAS & MCINTYRE   1985   VANCOUVER/TORONTO

To my grandparents
for their stories and their songs

Douglas & McIntyre Ltd.
1615 Venables Street
Vancouver, British Columbia

Canadian Cataloguing in Publication Data
Wallace, Ian, 1950-
    Chin Chiang and the dragon's dance
ISBN 0-88899-020-0
1. Chinese—Juvenile fiction.   I. Title.
PS8595.A5857C46 1984   jC813'.54   C83-098877-7
PZ7.W34Ch 1984

Printed and bound in Japan by Dai Nippon.
Second Printing, 1985

CHIN CHIANG AND THE DRAGON'S DANCE

From the time Chin Chiang stood only as high as his grandfather's knees, he had dreamed of dancing the dragon's dance. Now the first day of the Year of the Dragon had arrived and his dream was to come true. Tonight he would dance with his grandfather. But instead of being excited, Chin Chiang was so scared he wanted to melt into his shoes. He knew he could never dance well enough to make Grandfather proud of him.

He stopped sweeping the floor of his family's shop and looked into the street where his mother and father were busy with other shopkeepers, hanging up paper lanterns shaped like animals, fish and birds.

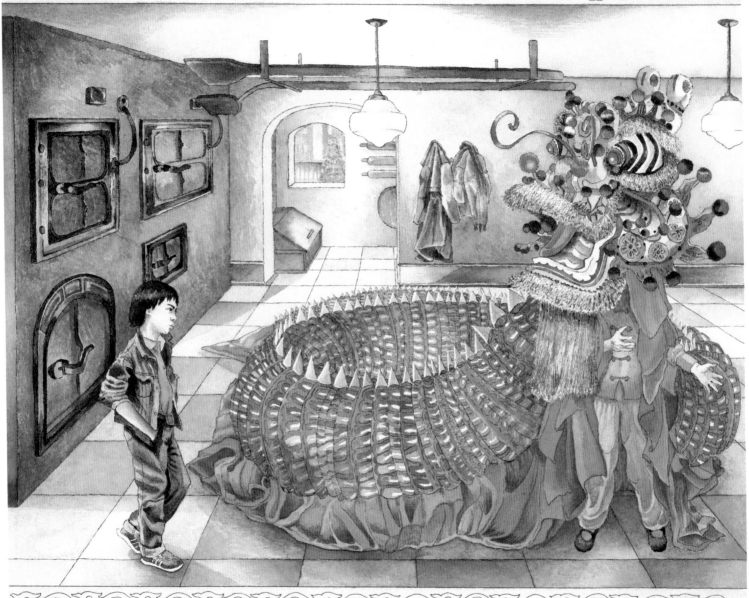

"It's time to practice our parts in the dragon's dance for the last time before the other dancers arrive, Chin Chiang. The afternoon is almost over," called Grandfather Wu from the bakeroom behind the shop.

"If I were a rabbit, I could run far away from here," Chin Chiang said to himself, "but then Mama, Papa and Grandfather really would be ashamed of me." So very slowly he walked into the bakeroom where Grandfather Wu stood waiting. He was wearing the splendid fierce dragon's head that he would put on again that night for the parade.

"Pick up the silk tail on the floor behind me," said his grandfather from inside the dragon's head, "and together we will be the most magnificent dragon that anyone has ever seen."

Chin Chiang did as he was asked, but as his grandfather started to dance, Chin Chiang did not move. "Grandfather can hide under the dragon's head," he whispered, "but if I trip or fall, I have nowhere to hide. Everyone will say, 'There goes clumsy Chin Chiang.'"

Grandfather Wu stopped dancing. "A dragon must have a tail as well as a head," he said gently.

Chin Chiang looked down at his shoes. "I can't dance the dragon's dance," he said.

"You have trained for a long time, Chin Chiang. Tonight, when you dance, you will bring tears of pride to your parents' eyes. Now come, join me and practice just as we have practiced before."

But when Chin Chiang tried to leap he tripped, stumbled and fell. Why had he ever thought he could dance the dragon's dance? Why had he ever wanted to? He was much too clumsy.

He jumped up and ran—away from his grandfather, out of the shop, into the market street. He stopped long enough to pick up a rabbit lantern, poke two holes for eyes and shove it over his head.

"Look, look. It's the dragon's tail!" called Mrs. Lau, dangling a speckled salmon for Chin Chiang to see. "Tonight, when you dance, the Great Dragon who lives in the clouds above the mountains will be honored, and next year he will fill our nets with beautiful fish like this."

Chin Chiang turned away.

"And he will grow oranges of a size and color never seen before," called Mr. Koo.

"What they say is true," added Mr. Sing. "The Great Dragon will bring prosperity and good fortune, if your dance pleases him."

But Chin Chiang remembered what one of the other dancers had once told him. If the dance was clumsy, the Great Dragon would be angry. Then he might toss the fruit from the trees and flood the valley. *It will all be my fault,* thought Chin Chiang. *Grandfather Wu will have to choose someone else to dance with him.* He waited to hear no more and raced across the market street.

"Our fish!" called Mrs. Lau.

"Our oranges!" called Mr. Koo.

Chin Chiang turned the corner.

"Our dance," called Grandfather Wu, from the doorway.

Looking out through the lantern, Chin Chiang hurried along the road by the sea to the public library, which he had visited many times when he wanted to be alone. He opened the door and ran up the stairs, round and round, higher and higher, up, up, up, to the door at the top that led out to the roof.

From his perch in the sky he could see the mountains rising above the sea and below him the animal lanterns, which would glow like tiny stars tonight. Chin Chiang felt happier than he had for many days.

"I never expected to meet a rabbit on top of this roof," called a strange voice.

Chin Chiang turned around quickly. A woman carrying a mop and pail was coming toward him.

"I'm not a rabbit," he said shyly. "I am Chin Chiang," and he pulled off the lantern.

"Oh, that is much better," she said. "Greetings, Chin Chiang. My name is Pu Yee. May I enjoy the view with you?" She didn't wait for a reply. "In a little while I'll be watching the New Year's parade from here. I used to dance the dragon's dance when I was young, but not any more. My feet are too old, and they are covered with corns."

"My grandfather dances the dragon's dance," said Chin Chiang, "and his corns are as old as yours."

Pu Yee laughed. "His old shoes may move his old bones, but my feet will never dance again."

A wonderful idea suddenly came to Chin Chiang. What if he had found someone to dance in his place? He would show Pu Yee his part in the dance right now. No one would see them if they tripped or fell. "You can help me practice what my grandfather taught me," he said.

"Oh, my creaky bones, what a funny sight that will be," said Pu Yee.

"You can dance," he told her. Cautiously Chin Chiang gave a little jump. Pu Yee jumped too. He shook slowly at first and she shook too. Next they leaped into the air, landed together and spun on their heels. Before long Pu Yee had forgotten her creaky bones. Then Chin Chiang stumbled and fell.

"Let's try again," said Pu Yee, picking him up.

While they danced, darkness had crept down slowly from the mountains to the city below. Then, from far off, Chin Chiang heard the lilting tune of pigeons with whistles tied to their tail feathers. They had been set free from their cages in the marketplace and were flying high above the buildings. Chin Chiang knew this meant that the New Year Festival had begun.

"We must go, Pu Yee. We're late," said Chin Chiang. "The pigeons are flying free."

"*I'm* not late," she replied. "I'm staying here."

But Chin Chiang pulled her by the hand, and they hurried down the stairs together—round and round, down, down, down, to the market street. The sound of firecrackers exploded in their ears while the eager crowd buzzed and hummed. Chin Chiang pushed his way forward, but Pu Yee pulled back. In the noise and confusion Chin Chiang let go of her hand, and suddenly he came face to face with the dragon whose head was wreathed in smoke.

"Where have you been, Chin Chiang? I have been sick with worry," called Grandfather Wu in a muffled voice. Chin Chiang did not reply. "Come now, take up the tail before the smoke disappears and everyone can see us."

Chin Chiang stood still, his feet frozen to the ground. The clamor of the street grew louder, stinging his ears. "I can't dance, Grandfather," he said.

Grandfather Wu turned away. "You can dance, Chin Chiang. Follow me."

"Look, look. Here comes the dragon!" called Mr. Sing. The crowd sent up a cheer that bounced off windows and doors and jumped into the sky.

Chin Chiang was trapped. Slowly he stooped and picked up the tail. Grandfather Wu shook the dragon's head fiercely until Chin Chiang started to kick up his heels to the beat of the thundering drum.

Then, suddenly, Chin Chiang stumbled, but instead of falling he did a quick step and recovered his balance. Excitedly, he leaped into the air, and again, and higher again. And as the dance went on, Chin Chiang's feet moved more surely, his steps grew firmer and his leaps more daring. Mrs. Lau and Mr. Koo cheered from their market shops while people poured out of their houses onto balconies and sidewalks, filling the streets. High in the sky flags of fire and falling moons burst into light. They sizzled and sparkled, rocketed straight up and whistled to the ground.

Just then Chin Chiang caught sight of a familiar face in the crowd. It was Pu Yee. Chin Chiang leaped to the sidewalk and pulled her into the street.

"I can't, Chin Chiang," she said, pulling away. "My bones. My corns. My knees."

"Pu Yee, yes, you can," Chin Chiang assured her. "Look at me!" Hesitantly she took hold of the tail and together they kicked up their heels just as they had on the rooftop, while the throngs of people cheered them on. Up one street and down another they danced, to the beat of the thundering drum.

All too soon the dragon lifted its head and shook its tail for the last time. The dance was over. Pu Yee hugged Chin Chiang close.

Grandfather Wu smiled inside the dragon's head. "Bring your new friend to our home for dinner, Chin Chiang," he said. Pu Yee and Chin Chiang hopped quickly over the doorstep and into the bakeshop.

The family exchanged gifts of fine teas in wooden boxes, new clothes and small red envelopes of Lucky Money. Then they sat together to share plates of meat dumplings and carp, bowls of steaming soup and trays of delicious pastries and cakes and fresh fruit.

"To Chin Chiang, the very best dragon's tail I have ever seen," said Grandfather Wu, raising his glass in a toast.

Chin Chiang's face glowed with pride. "To a prosperous Year of the Dragon," he said, raising his glass to his mama, papa, grandfather and his new friend Pu Yee.